For Lily and Willow

Published by Bloomsbury, New York and London
Distributed to the trade by St. Martin's Press
Printed in Singapore by Tien Wah Press
Library of Congress Cataloging-in-Publication Data
Robinson, Bruce.
The obvious elephant /
Bruce Robinson and Sophie Windham.—1st U.S. ed.
p.cm. Summary:
When an elephant appears one day in the town square, no one,
including the elephant itself, knows what it is.
[1. Elephants—Fiction.] I. Windham, Sophie, ill. II. Title
PZ7.R5645 Ob 2002
[E]—dc21
ISBN 1-58234-769-7
First U.S. Edition 2002
1 3 5 7 9 10 8 6 4 2
Bloomsbury Children's Books USA
175 Fifth Avenue
New York, NY 10010

THE OBVIOUS ELEPHANT

BY BRUCE ROBINSON   ILLUSTRATED BY SOPHIE WINDHAM

BLOOMSBURY
CHILDREN'S
BOOKS

NEW YORK

Imagine a town, in a country, where a simple thing like an Elephant had never been seen, or even heard of …

Well, not so long ago, there was a town exactly like that, and one day the people awoke to find an Elephant sitting bewildered in the main square, mopping his brow with a red spotted handkerchief and wondering how he got there.

At first the people were afraid of him. But he seemed so friendly that they soon lost their fear and went over to speak to him.

"What's your name?" they asked. "And what are you?"

"I don't know," said the Elephant. "And I don't have a name."

The people all looked confused. How could a thing as big as that have no name? And not know what it was?

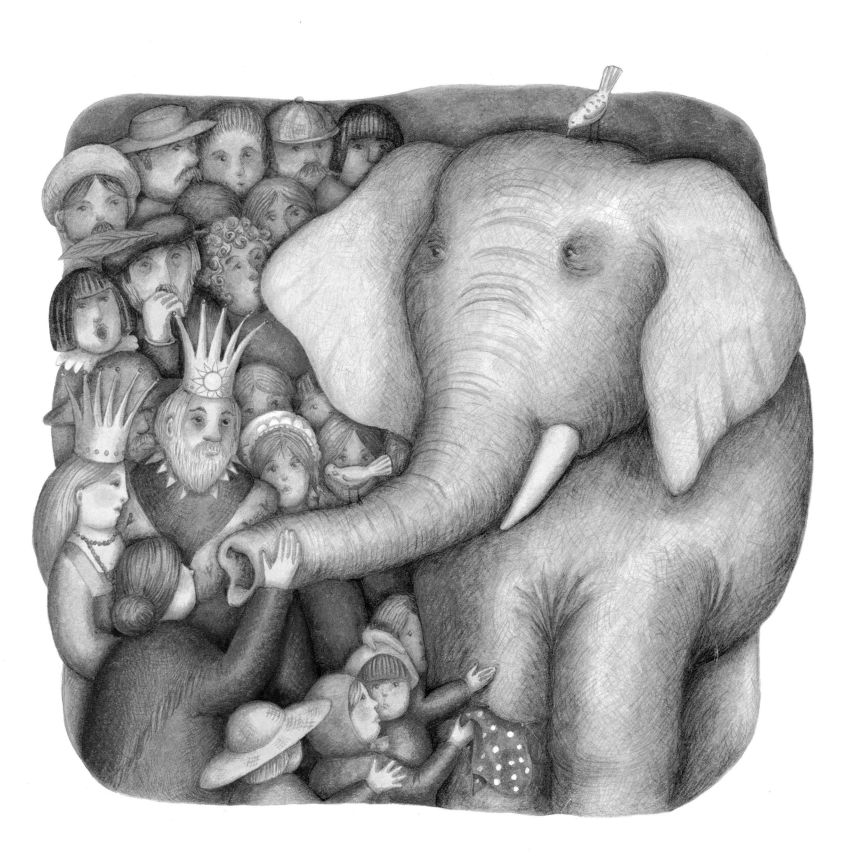

"You've got no business not to have a name," they said.

"You've got no business not knowing what you are!"

"I know what he is," said a little boy who was seven and three quarters and known for telling Tall Stories. His name, (which was embroidered on both his socks) was Eric, and no one ever listened to him.

"I know exactly what he is!" said Eric.

"Quiet," said the Policeman. "I'm going to poke him with this stick and see what he does."

The Policeman poked him and the Elephant didn't like it.

"Maybe it should be plugged in?" said someone.

"He's not electric," said Eric.

"Look at that nozzle on him," someone said. "What's that for?"

No one knew, except Eric, and no one was listening to him.

"All right, I've got it," said the Train Driver. "It's obvious what it is. It's a new type of railway engine."

So they took the Elephant to the railway station and connected him to a train. But he wouldn't move.

"Why doesn't he go?" asked everyone. "Give him some coal."

"But I don't like coal," said the Elephant. "I like cookies and cakes."

"If you like cookies and cakes," said the Train Driver, "then you can't be a train. I wonder what you could be."

"I'll tell you what he is," said Eric.

"Oh, do be quiet!" said the grown-ups.

"All right, it's obvious what he is," said the Fireman. "He's a fire engine. Look at his hose! That's what that long nozzle is. Give him to me, I'll put that fire out with him."

So they took the Elephant to the big fire and pointed him at the flames. But he didn't like it at all, and was frightened of the red and yellow blaze.

"Oh, no, no, no, no, no! He can't be a fire engine," said the Garbage Collector. "He doesn't like fire. But it's obvious what he is."

"What's that?" they all asked (except Eric, who knew).

"He is a modern type of trash collecting machine," said the Garbage Collector. "A type of vacuum cleaner."

So they took the Elephant around the streets to empty all the trash cans. But the Elephant sucked up so much garbage from them that he nearly burst!

"He's no good," they said. "He's a rotten thing whatever he is. He can't do anything."

The Elephant looked upset.

"But he must do something," said the Train Driver, the Fireman, and the Garbage Collector. "Let's take him to the Professor to examine."

The Elephant looked frightened.

"Don't worry," said Eric, holding up the great big ear to whisper. "The Professor is nice and anyway, I'll come with you."

"Will you?" said the Elephant.

"Of course I will," said Eric. "I'll look after you."

The Elephant was very happy to have a friend, and circling Eric with his trunk, lifted him up and put him on top of his head like a hat.

All eyes were looking up at Eric — it was a good place to sit — and off they all went to see the Professor.

"Interesting," said the Professor.
"Very interesting indeed."
He took measurements and photographs,
(some with Eric in them), made detailed drawings,
carried out scientific tests, and worked out plans.
At last he came to his conclusion.

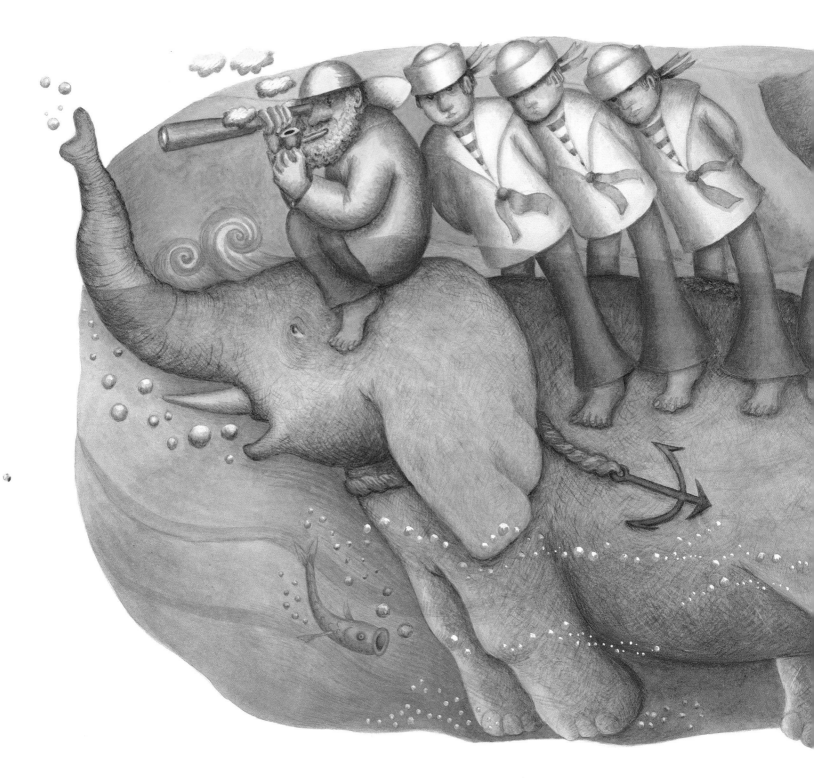

"At first," said the Professor, "I thought this great big enormous and quite huge thing might be a strange sort of submarine (it was the periscope that confused me), but after further research, and consultation with my friend the Driver, I now feel sure. I am confident to tell you, that it is ..."

"Yes?" they said.

"It is ..." said the Professor.

"Yes? Yes?"

"A big . . . um . . ." the Professor hesitated, trying to remember the word. "A big . . ."

"Yes? Yes? Yes?" they all said. "A big what?"

"Elephant!" shouted Eric, still on the Elephant's head.

"Yes," confirmed the Professor. "That's what it is! An Elephant, no more, no less."

"An Elephant?" they said. "What's that?"

"It is," said the Professor, "what you see in front of you."

"But what does it do?" they asked.

"It does nothing!" cried Eric. "It simply is an Elephant."

"Yes, of the long-nosed variety," added the Professor.

"Well," they said, "that makes all the difference. If he's an Elephant, he's an Elephant. We can't imagine why we didn't think of it before."

The people of the town were very proud and pleased with their Elephant, so pleased they built him a special house and garden in the park with a greenhouse to grow his vegetables — melons, carrots, cucumbers — which the Professor discovered was his proper food.

"Thank You for my lovely house," said the Elephant to all his guests at the moving-in party. "But if you wouldn't mind, there is one more thing I would like?"

"You can have anything," they said. "What is it?"

"A name," he replied.

"A name? Your name is Elephant."

"No it isn't," said the Elephant, "I want a proper name."

Everyone looked confused until Eric had an idea. Lifting the big ear, he put another whisper into it. He asked the Elephant if he could have a look at the red spotted handkerchief that he'd arrived with.

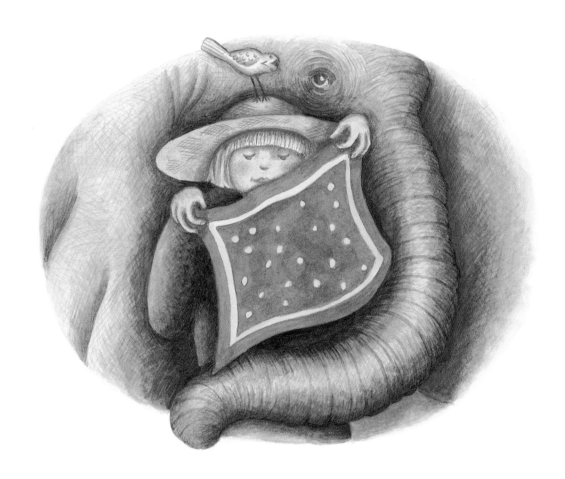

"I thought so!" he exclaimed. "Your name is embroidered on your handkerchief. If my socks are anything to go by, your name is Cotton!"

"It's obvious," everyone agreed, with a great round of applause. "His name is Cotton!"

Everybody was very happy. The whole town was very happy. And it Made Cotton and his new pal, Eric, very happy too.